I Can Learn Social Skills!

Poems About Getting Along, Being a Good Friend, and Growing Up

Benjamin Farrey-Latz

free spirit
PUBLISHING®

Library of Congress Cataloging-in-Publication Data
Names: Farrey-Latz, Benjamin, 1974– author.
Title: I can learn social skills! : poems about getting along, being a good friend, and growing up / by Benjamin Farrey-Latz.
Description: Minneapolis, MN : Free Spirit Publishing Inc., [2018] | Identifiers: LCCN 2018006852 (print) | LCCN 2018008287 (ebook) | ISBN 9781631982811 (Web PDF) | ISBN 9781631982828 (ePub) | ISBN 9781631982804 (pbk.) | ISBN 163198280X (pbk.)
Subjects: LCSH: Social skills in children—Juvenile literature. | Social skills—Juvenile literature.
Classification: LCC HQ783 (ebook) | LCC HQ783 .F37 2018 (print) | DDC 302/.14—dc23
LC record available at https://lccn.loc.gov/2018006852

Free Spirit Publishing does not have control over or assume responsibility for author or third-party websites and their content.

Reading Level Grade 3; Interest Level Ages 5–9;
Fountas & Pinnell Guided Reading Level O

Edited by Eric Braun
Cover and interior design by Emily Dyer

Photos and illustrations used throughout the book and on the cover are from Dreamstime and iStock.

10 9 8 7 6 5 4 3 2 1
Printed in China
R18860618

Free Spirit Publishing Inc.
6325 Sandburg Road, Suite 100
Minneapolis, MN 55427-3674
(612) 338-2068
help4kids@freespirit.com
www.freespirit.com

FSC
www.fsc.org
MIX
Paper from
responsible sources
FSC® C101537

Free Spirit offers competitive pricing.
Contact edsales@freespirit.com for pricing information on multiple quantity purchases.

Dedication

This book is dedicated to all my students—
past, present, and future.

Acknowledgments

I would like to thank many people for making this book a reality. Thank you to my amazing editor, Eric Braun, who helped me immensely in shaping and improving all the poems. Thank you to everyone at Free Spirit for all the work put into creating this book. Thank you to my colleagues and friends who read and gave feedback on early drafts of the poems. Thank you to my students, who inspired many of these poems. Thank you to all my teachers and professors who have helped me. Thank you to my parents and family for their support and excitement. A huge thank you to Brian for his support and encouragement and for his additional editing of many drafts along the way.

Contents

Poems About Behavior

Poems About Being a Good Friend

Building Social Skills with Poems:
Tips for Teachers, Parents, and Caregivers

I Can Do That!

I can stay calm when I am mad
And cheer you up when you feel sad.
I can have a snack to eat
And keep the table looking neat.

I can be honest and say what's true,
And I can learn to listen to you.
I can try hard to run really fast—
And still be okay if I come in last.

I can share and be a friend to you.
Together, let's see what we can do!

I Can Greet You!

Hi Hiya

How are you?

Doin' good—how 'bout you?

Feeling great, glad to say. Thanks for brightening my day!

Wow! I said hello and so did you.
I smiled at you and you smiled too.

Help, Please

Today we're learning a lot that's new,
But I feel lost—what should I do?
The teacher used words that I don't know,
Describing things from long ago.

I raise my hand
So the teacher can see
Something is
Confusing me.

"I don't understand," I say—
And my teacher helps me on my way.

Look 'em in the Eye

It's hard to look you in the eye.
It makes me nervous—I don't know why.

I'm actually listening to what you say
Even if I'm looking away.

But you can't tell, you think I don't care.
You say, "I'm here, not over there."

I think I know what I can do
To show that I'm interested in you.

I'll look at your nose, or just to the side.
It will seem like I'm looking you in the eye!

Keeping your face right in my view
Shows that I want to listen to you.

Can You Hear Me Now?

HEY GUYS, WHAT'S UP?

Did you see that show about those trucks?
I love the one with the racing stripes and the—

Wait—where are you going?

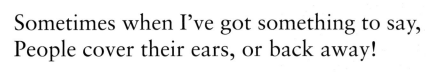

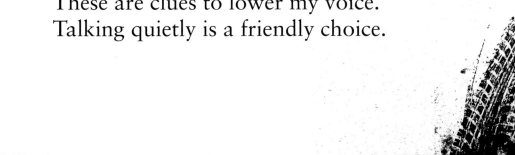

Sometimes when I've got something to say,
People cover their ears, or back away!

These are clues to lower my voice.
Talking quietly is a friendly choice.

My Turn to Talk

When others are talking
   and I want to talk too,
I listen to them
   until they're through.

They hear me better
   when I *wait* to speak,
And they're happier to
   hang out with me.

10

Game Time

You say I'm **OUT**.

I say I'm **IN**.

You say I **LOSE**.

I say I **WIN**.

It's hard for me to lose, you see—
Winning means a lot to me.
But if I fight or cheat or whine
Nobody has a very good time.

I know I can't win every game.
Having fun is the real aim.
And if I play fair in a spirit of fun,
The game's a good time for everyone.

I want other kids to ask me to join in
So I'll be a good sport—
        and then all of us win!

I'm Here!

He shouts and barrels into the room,
Slamming the door with a giant **BOOM**.

His classmates are startled. They look up and grumble,
Their work interrupted, their thoughts in a jumble.

"Please stop your stomping and yelling and thudding!
Come in more quietly while we are studying."

Tip-toe, tip-toe, tip-toe.

When you enter the room
With hardly a sound
You show respect
For the others around.

15

Lunchtime Gross-Out

Chomp, slurp, dribble, clack,
gobble sloppy lip SMACK!

I tear my food up when I eat,
The crumbs fall all around my feet.
I use my hands to squish and squeeze
My bread and cheese and mushy peas.

When I'm disgusting with my food
My friends say, "Wow, that's so gross, dude!"
I need to use my fork and spoon
And not eat like a wild raccoon.

I'll keep my mouth closed when I chew—
And clean things up when I am through!

Where Do My Hands Go?

Where do my hands go?

In my nose?
My friends and teachers say that's gross
And they don't like to be too close.

In my pants?
If my fingers find their way down there
This makes people stop and stare.

Others say that it looks wrong
When they see my hands where they don't belong.
When kids or grown-ups are in sight,
My hands and I can be polite.

Instead I'll let my fingers rest
Or squeeze a fidget on my desk.

How Can I Get Calm?

My heart is clattering in my chest.
My breath comes hard, my brain can't rest.
I'm like a rocket ready to blast!
I need to slow down and relax.

I take deep breaths
and count to ten.
Breathe in through my nose
and out again.
I tighten my muscles with a squeeze
and then relax them all with ease.

When I use all my calming tools,
My days are better at home and at school.

I Can Stay on Task

In class it's time for work to begin,

But I just want to **JUMP** or **SPIN**

My friend sits quietly in her chair—
She focuses on her work with care.

Hmmm . . .

I know what she'll do when she's done:
She'll play on the slide and have some fun.
So I'll work quietly, and when I'm through
I'll go outdoors, and I'll slide too!

Who's There?

KNOCK-KNOCK!

Ha ha!

What do you call a . . . ?

Get it?

If you want to be one of the funny folks,
But you don't always know the right time for jokes,

Listen and look at what others do—
Are they acting goofy too?

Is the teacher laughing, or is she frowning?
Does *everyone* think it's time for clowning?

If not, then save that joke for later—
The one with the running refrigerator.

Make the Switch

I'm busy with something I love to do:
Coloring all the flowers blue.

A few more to go—I'm almost done.
Choice time today is super fun!

"Time to STOP"? What does she mean?!
I still have to color all the leaves green.

"You can finish that later," she says to me.
"Right now we're having a spelling bee."

So . . .

I'll put my flowers and crayons away
And save them for another day.

When it's time to move on, I know I can do it.
It feels good to know that I can work through it.

Math: 8:30

Storytime: 9:20

Recess: 10:00

Science: 10:40

Art: 11:30

Lunch: 12:15

Gym: 1:00

Change Is So Hard

A field trip or a classroom guest.
An assembly or a reading test.

Many things can disrupt my day.
Making me grumpy right away.

My routines mean a lot to me—
I like to have consistency.

But I tell myself,
    "Breathe deep, stay cool.
Sometimes things are
    different at school."

When changes pop up,
    I've learned to stay calm.
It might be a challenge,
    but I can move on.

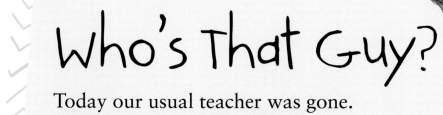

Who's That Guy?

Today our usual teacher was gone.
A substitute was in her place.
The new guy got the schedule wrong,
And did science in the reading space.

He couldn't remember all of our names,

His storytime voices weren't the same,

And he didn't know our favorite games!

Though it can be hard when so much is new,
When we have a sub, we know what to do:
Even when things don't go as planned,
We're patient, we listen, and we lend a hand.

You Have Feelings Too?

My side

Your side

His side

Her side

My way's the way we should have tried.
Listen to me!
Can't you see?
That's how things should always be!

But that's
not how
it works.

I'll learn to hear your point of view
And try to see things like you do.

I have feelings, and you do too!
I want to know what matters to you.

What do *you* say?
What is *your* way?
Understanding others can make their day.

I Wait and Wait and . . .

I don't like to wait my turn.
Patience is so hard to learn!

Grown-ups say I'll get my chance soon . . .
But sometimes it feels like I wait
        and wait
                and wa-a-a-a-ait—
all afternoon.

                ARGH! What can I do?

Squeeze a squeeze ball?
    Squish, squeeze, squish, squeeze

Count to myself?
    One two three, one two three

Look at a book?
    Long ago, in a boat at sea . . .

It's hard to wait, that much is true.
But I'll keep myself busy
            —and be patient too!

Anxious

What are the tools that I can use
When I'm anxious and nervous and stressed?

When the worries inside
Make me wish I could hide
From the tension I feel in my chest?

When my heart pounds and pounds
And I'm breathing too hard?
When my thoughts run around
And my body's on guard?

I can pause and wipe the sweat off my brow,
And talk about how I feel right now.

I can stretch down to the ground and then up like a tree,
And take some deep breaths: one . . . two . . . three.

I tell myself that I'm okay
As I calm myself in a healthy way.

Mad

It's hard to control my hands and feet—
I want to yell and kick and punch!
My face turns red with angry heat
As I thrash, and hit, and smash my lunch.

It's okay to be angry, but something I know
Is that losing control can make me feel low.
It can make my friends want to stay away—
Or argue and fight instead of play.

So I'll slowly count from one to ten,
Breathe in deep, then out again.
I'll go for a run or maybe a walk.
Or I'll jump, or rest, or say, "Can we talk?"

I'll stop, and think, and use my tools
Until I feel more calm and cool.

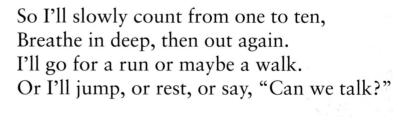

Poke

Poke, grab, rub
Tickle, hit, hug
Nudge, hold, scratch, and tug—

Oops!
I touch other kids
Even when they say **STOP**.
How annoying it is
When I poke, prod, and chop!

40

I'll find something else for my fingers to do.
Like rub them together, two by two,
Squish some clay or squeeze a ball,
Do a puzzle or hug a doll.

With my hands to myself I can still have fun,
And that will be better for everyone!

TooClose!

I'm excited when I see someone I know—
And I come so close that we're toe-to-toe!
But some people grumble, "Get outta my face,"
Or ask me to give them a little more space.

I don't always know how far to stay,
So I'll start with being an arm's length away.
I won't get so close that others think, "Whoa!"
I'll find the right distance and that's where I'll go.

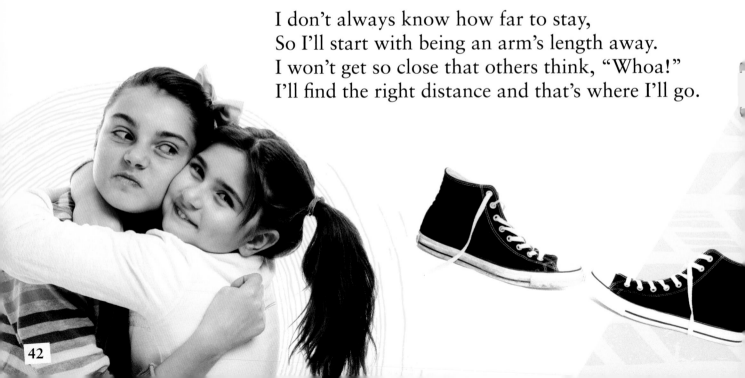

43

Yes, I Did It

When I'm in a conflict with my friend
I might want to blame him till the end.

But I know it's best to admit my part
And say I'm sorry—from the heart.

When I hurt someone with what I do or say,
I want to fix it in an honest way—
Not just with words, but with actions too.
To make it right, here's what I'll do:

I say, "I'm sorry"—that's how I begin.
I resolve to be kinder than I have been.

If I said something mean, I'll say something nice.
If I did something wrong, I'll try to do right.

An apology means I'll fix what I can
And I promise I won't hurt you again.

Building Social Skills with Poems: Tips for Teachers, Parents, and Caregivers

Learning social skills can be challenging for students of all ages. As adults, we often can forget that things like understanding emotions, handling strong feelings, using manners, and displaying appropriate behavior in different situations can be subtle and not always obvious to children. These skills are important not only to help students get along with one another and adults, but also to help them succeed—at school, at home, and everywhere else.

Poetry can be a fun and memorable way for younger kids to explore these important lessons. And rhyming has been shown to aid in retention of information. You can share *I Can Learn Social Skills!* with students as part of a larger social skills lesson or on its own.

How to Use the Poems

You may want to read several poems with your group as a way to introduce social skills in general. This could prompt discussions about areas in which students need to improve their skills. More often, you will probably read individual poems that apply to specific situations or skills. For example, if you have students who experience anxiety or who don't like change, you could read "Anxious," "Change Is So Hard," and "Look 'em in the Eye" or "Make the Switch." The poems are grouped into categories to make it easier to find the skills you want to teach, but many poems can apply to multiple situations or skills.

Read the poems aloud and ask children to recite them back. Assign students to memorize poems, or do role plays in which children (and adults) act out scenes from the poems. Most important of all, talk about the poems. Ask students what the message is. Ask if they have ever struggled with similar issues. How have they solved these struggles in the past? What other solutions can they think of?

Of course, the social skills messages embedded in these poems are best learned when students also practice the skills the poems discuss. Try the following activities along with the poems to give children opportunities to apply what they've learned.

"I Can Do That!"

This poem introduces the topic of social skills, with an emphasis on the ideas that social skills are about the things we do together and that all of us can learn and strengthen these skills. Playing off the poem's title, brainstorm with students to come up with a list of things they can already do, as well as things they would like to be able to do. This list can be set up as a T-chart on paper or on a chalkboard or whiteboard. Help guide the discussion at first by suggesting simple tasks (at school or outside of school) students may or may not be able to do. Then move on to social skills, suggesting ideas such as "I can be a good friend," "I can listen to other people," or "I can calm myself down when I am mad." If it's appropriate and safe for your group and environment, children can show some of the things they can do. Talk about how doing these things might affect others.

Poems About Talking with Others

The first three poems in this section can be helpful to students who tend to be on the quieter side or who need to learn to self-advocate.

"I Can Greet You"

Use this poem as a jumping-off point for brainstorming different types of greetings. List verbal greetings, such as "Hello," "Hi," "How are you?" and "How's it going?" Then have students think of nonverbal greetings, such as a nod, smile, wave, or fist bump. Take it a step further by role-playing situations where people meet and greet each other.

"Help, Please"

This poem reminds students that adults may not realize students need help if children don't ask for it. After reading, ask students to talk about a time they needed help and did or did not ask for it. If they didn't ask for help, why not? If they did, what happened? Role-play asking for help in different situations, such as:

- A teacher is explaining how to complete a math problem and you don't understand the information.

- A parent or teacher gives you directions on how to clean up, but you don't understand the directions.

- You are being teased on the playground and aren't sure what to do.

"Look 'em in the Eye"

Some children don't feel comfortable looking others directly in the eye, which can be an important way to signal our interest and engagement. Be sure, however, to take cultural differences into account when teaching this skill. For example, direct eye contact is seen as courteous in some cultures, but in others it is considered impolite. Also, students with special needs who may be uneasy with direct eye contact can at least learn to look in someone's direction. Students can practice greeting others and either looking them in the eye or looking nearby, to the side of the person's face or nose. Older children could be encouraged to discuss how eye contact makes them feel.

"Can You Hear Me Now?" and "My Turn to Talk"

Many students need reminders about respectfully participating in conversation, which is the focus of these two poems. Model different volumes of talking (for example, quiet, inside voice, loud) and ask children to decide if you are speaking "too soft," "just right," or "too loud." Then turn it around and ask students to try speaking at different volumes in groups or pairs while others report if the child is speaking "too soft," "just right," or "too loud."

Appropriate voice volume also depends on the situation. Ask students to give examples of when it is appropriate to use each of the volumes (quiet, inside voice, loud). Practice the best volumes for different settings, such as the classroom, library, lunchroom, gymnasium, or playground at school. (It's most effective if you can actually bring children to each of these places to practice, but if that is not practical, it's worthwhile to role-play using appropriate voice volume in different environments.) At home, parents can practice at the dinner table, in the living room, in the bedroom, in the hallway, and outside. Appropriate voice volume also may vary depending on whether you live in a house versus an apartment building, who lives in the home, and what time of day it is.

You can also role-play conversations, asking kids to determine the right time to join in. You may need to coach them on waiting for breaks in the discussion and being aware of other people's social cues.

Poems About Manners

The poems in this section include a variety of lessons about socializing and getting along with others, from playing fair to keeping your hands where they belong.

"Game Time"

You could read this poem daily before recess, playtime, team sports, or other group activities at school or home. Children may benefit from the reminder that it's important that they try to have a good time (and help others have a good time) even if they don't win. Have students talk or write about an experience when they or someone they know was more interested in winning than in having fun. How did that change the tone of the game? (Be sure to tell students *not* to name names or use details that would clearly identify a specific person if they are talking about another child.)

"I'm Here!"

You can use this poem together with "Can You Hear Me Now?" to practice appropriate volume when speaking. Students can also model coming into a room politely in different situations: after recess, coming back from another classroom, and coming from lunch or the media center. At home, children can practice coming through the door, coming into a room for mealtime, and so on. With older students, you could discuss the idea of "reading the room"— looking at social and environmental cues to understand the mood of a room and adjusting their behavior as they come in.

"Lunchtime Gross-Out"

Consider reading this poem daily before or after lunch as a reminder to eat neatly and clean up after oneself. For a fun role play, set up a special meal in the classroom (or at home) where children can practice using different utensils. During snack time, have children practice eating politely, using their manners, and cleaning up. It can also be fun and informative to have students demonstrate manners for different settings or situations. Of course, as adults, we always want to model appropriate mealtime manners.

"Where Do My Hands Go?"

Many students need a reminder of what they may and may not do with their hands. Younger children may need to be taught to blow their noses. Some students may not realize it's considered gross by other people when students pick their noses or put their hands in their pants. It's important not to shame or embarrass students for these behaviors, but to show them what else they can do in these situations: use a tissue to blow your nose, fold your hands in your lap, ask to use the bathroom if you have an itch in an uncomfortable or private spot. As a class, discuss public versus private behaviors.

Poems About Behavior

Poems in this section include tips for helping children regulate their behavior and stay calm in different situations. It's helpful to practice calming tools when children are already calm so that when they are feeling strong emotions, they will have already had some experience successfully using these strategies.

"How Can I Get Calm?" "Make the Switch," "Change Is So Hard," and "Who's That Guy?"

All these poems involve avoiding a meltdown in different situations. Here are some role-play starters to get students working on using their calming tools when faced with anxiety, unexpected changes, and transitions. In these role plays, have one child play the student while another plays the teacher, whose role is to reassure the student. If students are not able to role-play the teacher, based on your knowledge of your group, then you can step in and "play" the teacher yourself in these scenarios.

- **Field trip:** Pretend the class is going to an art museum and a student has never been there before. The student is nervous and doesn't know what to do. The teacher can help the student by explaining what she doesn't know or understand (for example, look at the art but don't touch and use a respectful volume in the museum). Students can also practice asking for the help they need.

- **Surprise assembly:** Pretend the class is about to go to the auditorium for a special assembly where the music teacher will lead students in some new songs. It is not the usual time for an assembly, and the student is very upset. The teacher can tell the student what will be happening in the assembly and can let him know when he will be able to complete the activities he'd normally be doing during that time. If the activity is not able to be made up later, the teacher and student can practice self-coaching: "Oh, well. It's different today. It may be hard for me, but I can handle a change once in a while." Or, "It's okay that I am uncomfortable. I will do my best with the change."

- **Substitute teacher:** In this role play, students are surprised by a substitute teacher in class, and some students feel stress when the sub doesn't follow the usual class procedures. Students can practice respectfully explaining to the sub how things are usually done. They can also practice accepting something different, using examples from the poem "Who's That Guy?" For example, the sub announces an activity that's not normally on the schedule. Have a student question this change, and have the sub hold firm on it. Then students can practice calmly moving on from the change: "It's just for today. Our teacher will be back soon."

- **Changing activities before finishing the first activity:** Students can role-play coloring or playing a game when the teacher tells them it's time to do math. They can practice putting the coloring sheet or game in a safe place in the room and then going to their math spots.

"I Can Stay on Task" and "Who's There?"

These two poems give students some reminders of appropriate classroom behaviors. When discussing the poems, give each student two cards—one that says "Yes" and one that says "No."

For "I Can Stay on Task," give examples or show pictures of children who are on or off task. Students hold up the "Yes" card if they think the child is on task and the "No" card if they think the child is off task. For "Who's There?" give examples of appropriate and inappropriate times to tell a joke in class. Have students hold up their "Yes" cards if they think it's an appropriate time and their "No" cards if they think it's not appropriate. Discuss why each situation is or is not appropriate.

To go further with the topic of staying on task, lead a discussion about the challenges and benefits of working hard during deskwork time. Acknowledge that it is not always easy to stay on task, especially when you would prefer to be doing something else. Why should students try to stay focused? What are the rewards of doing so? You might draw comparisons to other areas of students' lives, such as practicing at sports or even staying focused on a video game. Does their focus in those cases help them improve their skills?

For a fun activity related to "Who's There?" ask for volunteers to share a joke and talk about when they first heard it. Was it an appropriate time? When have *they* told the joke before? How did people react?

You can also have students write or draw about these topics.

Poems About Being a Good Friend

Many of the poems in this section are about empathy and understanding that our actions impact other people.

"You Have Feelings Too?"

This poem reminds children that other people have feelings. Put students in pairs and have them draw pictures of each other feeling different emotions. You can also have students play a game in which they guess the emotion the other person is modeling. Provide students with emotions to show or invite them to come up with their own ideas.

"I Wait and Wait and . . ."

This poem reminds us that waiting can be hard. Lead a discussion in which children talk about what kinds of things are hard for them to wait for at school, at home, or in their communities. Next, invite students to role-play waiting for different things, such as:

- having a question answered by the teacher

- reaching the front of the lunch line

- checking out at a store with a family member

- getting a turn to play a game

- meeting a friend who is late

During or after each role play, prompt students to consider what they can do to make it easier for them to wait patiently. For example, while waiting for the teacher to answer a question, students could work on other problems. While waiting in line at lunch or at a store, they could play a quiet game like I spy. And while waiting for someone who is late, they could do some quick exercises like jumping jacks or running in place.

"Anxious" and "Mad"

As with "You Have Feelings Too?" students can do activities involving drawing or modeling the emotions described in these poems. These poems are also an opportunity for students to practice their calming tools: deep breaths, counting to 10, walking away, playing with a fidget, using calming self-talk, and so on. Have students write about a time they got anxious or mad and how they dealt with it, or ask for volunteers to share with the class.

Another option you might offer students is to sit on large exercise balls (if you have them available) instead of chairs. This can be a great calming strategy, because it allows students to move while at their desks or tables. This option can even help some students focus better on schoolwork since they are able to move and self-calm in a way that is not distracting to others.

"Poke"

This poem reminds students that other people don't always want to be touched. As a group, brainstorm various kinds of friendly touch, such as patting, high-fiving, or hugging another person. Then role-play asking for permission to touch someone this way and accepting the other person's answer. If the answer is *no*, don't touch. If it's *yes*, give the other person the pat, high five, or hug. It's also important to teach or remind students that certain types of touch are never okay, even if the other person says yes. Teach children the "swimsuit rule": We don't touch anyone anywhere that would be covered by a swimsuit.

"TooClose!"

Have each student draw and color in a red circle on one piece of paper and a green circle on another piece. (Alternatively, students can make these colored circles using a drawing program on a computer.) If you like, you may glue the circles onto cardboard or tagboard to make them sturdier. To help students understand physical space and boundaries, have them stand in two lines facing each other. The students in one line slowly walk toward the people across from them. The children in the second line hold up their green circles until they feel the other person is getting too close. Then they switch to the red circle. The lines could then switch roles. Point out that "too close" is different for different people.

"Yes, I Did It" and "Fix It"

Have a group discussion about conflict and apologizing. Talk about the steps to an apology:

1. Admit to the person what you did.

2. Say or write to the person that you are sorry.

3. Come up with a way to fix the situation.

As a group, brainstorm a list of potential conflicts between students that would require someone to apologize for what he or she did. Then have students write the three steps to an apology using the specifics of the conflict, describing it in their own words and coming up with their own ideas for how to fix it.

Ask for volunteers to share what they wrote. Examples of conflicts might be hitting, breaking someone's belonging, taking a toy without asking, and not including someone in a game or other activity. Examples of fixing conflict include:

- promising not to be hurtful in the future ("Instead of hitting, I will use my words to say why I'm mad or will walk away and come back when I can talk without hitting.")

- fixing or replacing something you broke (or, if the item cannot be fixed or replaced, perhaps sharing another toy)

- inviting someone to play

- making an apology that includes a card or picture

Lead a group discussion about why it can be hard to apologize—and why it's important to do so anyway. Point out that the poem "Yes, I Did It" is only four lines long and doesn't actually show the speaker "doing" anything. So what do students think the title means?

Regardless of which poems you're working on as a group, it can be fun and valuable to invite children to write their own poems. These might be on topics similar to the poems you're reading together or on topics of students' own choosing. Invite children to illustrate their poems, and hang them in the classroom or hall. Or, bind the poems into a book to produce a class poetry anthology.

Read stories about related social skills and help students make connections between the stories and these poems. For example, did the character in the story use the skill the poem describes? What would have happened if the character had acted differently? Talk about how students think the characters in the stories feel and how those characters might feel differently if specific social skills had been used (or not used).

I would love to hear your stories of how you used these poems in your classroom or with your group. You can reach me at help4kids@freespirit.com.

—Benjamin

About the Author

Benjamin Farrey-Latz is a special education teacher at Jefferson Community School (grades 2–6) in the Minneapolis School District. He has worked in education since 1996 in private, public, and charter schools as both a general education and special education teacher. After working several years in elementary education, Benjamin went back to school to become a special education teacher, completing the master's program at the University of Minnesota. His master's thesis focused on methods of teaching social skills to children with special needs.

Other Great Books from Free Spirit

I Like Being Me
Poems about kindness, friendship, and making good choices
by Judy Lalli, M.S.
64 pp.; B&W photos and color illust.; paperback; 8" x 8".
Ages 4–8.

Jamie Is Jamie
A Book About Being Yourself and Playing Your Way
by Afsaneh Moradian, illustrated by Maria Bogade
32 pp.; color illust.; hardcover; 8" x 8".
Ages 4–8.

Zach Apologizes
by William Mulcahy, illustrated by Darren McKee
32 pp.; color illust.; hardcover, 8" x 8".
Ages 5–8.

Tessie Tames Her Tongue
A Book About Learning When to Talk and When to Listen
by Melissa Martin, illustrated by Charles Lehman
36 pp.; color illust.; hardcover; 8" x 10".
Ages 5–9.

Cool Down and Work Through Anger
by Cheri J. Meiners, M.Ed., illustrated by Meredith Johnson
40 pp.; color illust.; paperback; 9" x 9".
Ages 4–8.

Voices Are Not for Yelling
by Elizabeth Verdick, illustrated by Marieka Heinlen
40 pp.; color illust.; paperback; 9" x 9".
Ages 4–7.

Interested in purchasing multiple quantities and receiving volume discounts?
Contact edsales@freespirit.com or call 1.800.735.7323 and ask for Education Sales.

Many Free Spirit authors are available for speaking engagements, workshops, and keynotes.
Contact speakers@freespirit.com or call 1.800.735.7323.

For pricing information, to place an order, or to request a free catalog, contact:

Free Spirit Publishing Inc. • 6325 Sandburg Road, Suite 100 • Minneapolis, MN 55427-3674
toll-free 800.735.7323 • local 612.338.2068 • fax 612.337.5050
help4kids@freespirit.com • www.freespirit.com